Emma Thomson's

felicity Wishes®

FELICITY WISHES: COOKING MAGIC
by Emma Thomson

British Library Cataloguing in Publication Data
A catalogue record of this book is available from the British Library.
ISBN 0-340-89340-0
Felicity Wishes © 2000 Emma Thomson.
Licensed by White Lion Publishing.
Felicity Wishes: Cooking Magic © 2005 Emma Thomson.

The right of Emma Thomson to be identified as the author
and illustrator of this Work has been asserted by WLP
in accordance with the Copyright, Designs and Patents Act 1988.

First HB edition published 2005
10 9 8 7 6 5 4 3 2

Published by Hodder Children's Books, a division of Hodder Headline Limited,
338 Euston Road, London, NW1 3BH

Printed in China

Emma Thomson's
felicity Wishes®

Cooking Magic

Hodder
Children's
Books

A division of Hodder Headline Limited

Felicity Wishes was full of sparkling excitement. It was Saturday morning and the start of a weekend cookery course that was being held at the School of Nine Wishes. What was even more sparkletastic was that the teacher was none other than celebrity chef Jenny Olivia!

"You're late!" whispered Polly to her best friend as Felicity skidded to a halt beside her. "And I can see why!"

It looked as though Felicity had brought the entire contents of her fairy kitchen, except the sink!

COOKERY
CLASS
REGISTRATION

"Welcome fairies!" called Jenny Olivia, as she tapped her wooden wand spoon on the table.

"It's really her!" whispered Felicity, completely starstruck.

"Cooking is a magical thing," Jenny Olivia began. "When you cook something that is made with love it has the amazing ability to transform into something special."

"I can't wait to get started!" said Felicity, eagerly unpacking her bags.

"It's wonderful that you're all so keen," continued Jenny looking at Felicity, "but it's important that we start at the beginning."

BASIC RULES

- 🧁 Tie your hair back.
- 🧁 Always wash your hands before you begin.
- 🧁 Protect your clothes with an apron.
- 🧁 Wear oven gloves when handling hot items.
- 🧁 Read the recipe through before you start.

Felicity was finding it hard to concentrate. It was the fourth time in five minutes that she had found herself looking up at the clock.

"There's so much theory!" she groaned, chewing the end of her pen.

"It's important to know what each piece of equipment does if you want to learn how to become a really magical chef," said Polly, with her head in a book.

"Hmmmm," replied Felicity dreamily, drifting away from the classroom to a place where she was the greatest chef in the whole of Fairy World.

After the long morning, Jenny Olivia had prepared a special picnic lunch to have under the Large Oak Tree. Felicity and her friends had never seen such mouth-watering food before.

"I can't wait to start cooking tomorrow and make yummy things like this!" said Holly, tucking into a star-shaped sandwich.

"Tomorrow?!" exclaimed Felicity, with her mouth full of cupcake.

"Weren't you listening?" Polly said disapprovingly. "The recipe for tomorrow's class is on the board and you were supposed to copy it down."

"Ooops!" said Felicity, flying off in a flutter.

EASY PICNIC FOOD

🧁 Make magical sandwiches by removing the crusts and using a cookie cutter to cut them into different shapes.

🧁 Decorate fairy cakes with something different. Add cherries, sprinkles, chocolate flakes or sweet sugary icing.

Felicity sat in the empty classroom scribbling down the recipe. Tomorrow seemed too long to wait to cook.

"I'm sure I've got enough ingredients here to make something wonderful," she said to herself as she picked up a cookery book titled 'The Experienced Fairy Chef'.

Felicity quickly found the perfect recipe.

"I'm only a couple of items short," she said, reading the recipe for a huge fluffy soufflé, "but I'm sure it won't matter."

In a whirl of flour and eggs, Felicity started to cook. Soon every utensil had been used and every surface covered.

After what seemed like a fairy lifetime, the soufflé was finally ready.

WHAT NOT TO DO TIPS

🧁 Don't use the same utensil for different things.

🧁 Don't leave boiling pans unattended.

🧁 Don't put anything in the oven until it's reached the correct temperature.

🧁 Don't eat raw mixture.

If Felicity had wanted to make a flat pancake she would have been happy with the result, but a perfectly flat soufflé was not what she had in mind!

"Oh my goodness," came a loud voice as Jenny Olivia and the other fairies returned.

Felicity winced in preparation for a telling-off.

"This is actually quite good!" said Jenny Olivia unexpectedly.

Felicity looked quizzically down at her soufflé pancake.

"It's perfect for teaching you all the final lesson in becoming a successful fairy chef – cleaning up!"

JENNY'S TOP CLEANING TIPS

🧁 Wash up as you go along.

🧁 Empty the bin as soon as it gets full.

🧁 Use separate cloths for the floor, surfaces, and washing up.

The next day Felicity was the first to arrive. Sheepishly, she shuffled to a seat at the back of the classroom.

Jenny Olivia looked up and smiled at Felicity.

"Don't worry about yesterday," she said kindly. "Enthusiasm, just like love, is an essential ingredient in making something yummy, and I think you're a natural!"

Felicity beamed as the room filled with excited fairies carrying bags of delicious ingredients to make Chunky Choc Treats.

HOW TO STIR IN LOVE

♡ Close your eyes and think of something that makes you happy.

♡ Wave the spoon over the top of the bowl.

♡ Stir the mixture three times to the right and three times to the left.

♡ Finish by tapping the spoon twice on the edge of the bowl.

Felicity's Gorgeously Gooey
Chunky Choc Treats

Ingredients:

350g/12oz chocolate spread
400g/14oz condensed milk
225g/8oz broken digestive biscuits

50g/2oz raisins
115g/4oz dried apricots
50g/2oz hazelnuts
Paper cake cases

Put the chocolate spread and condensed milk into a large mixing bowl.

Stir together until well mixed. Carefully blow six kisses into the bowl.

Add the biscuits, raisins, apricots and nuts and mix well until all the ingredients are coated in chocolate. Stir in some love (see opposite page for instructions).

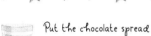

Put one generous tablespoonful of mixture in each paper case. Use your wooden spoon like a wand to plant a happy wish on top of each treat.

Put the treats in the fridge for 2 hours while you lick the bowl and do the washing up.

Share your treats with everyone who is special to you.

Sweet chocolate smells filled the air as freshly made Chunky Choc Treats were displayed on the table.

"Just because something looks good doesn't mean it will taste good," said Jenny Olivia to the class. "To receive your Cookery Club Certificate your chocolate bars will have to pass the taste test. Please can I have a volunteer?"

Before anyone could put their hand up there was the most enormous loud tummy rumble.

"Felicity!" said Jenny Olivia. "It looks as though you are hungry enough to be the judge!"

Felicity licked her lips as she delicately took a fairy size bite of the first treat.

"They're all delicious," she said when she came to the last plate, "in fact, they are pure fairy magic!"

Certificate of Cooking Magic

This is to certify that

Felicity Wishes

has excelled in the following cooking skills:

✶ Learning and remembering to use the basic rules.
✶ Developing a good knowledge of essential cooking equipment.
✶ Demonstrating cleanliness and hygiene in the kitchen.
✶ Making delicious fairy food with love.

signed
Jenny Olivia

With this book on
Cooking Magic comes a
shimmery Felicity wish:

Open the book with your eyes closed
and let it fall open on any page.
Think of a wish you'd always dreamed
would come true and whisper it into the
page three times.

Keep this book in a safe place and,
maybe, one day, your wish
might just come true.

Love felicity
x